by Marc Brown

Parents Magazine Press
New York

Library of Congress Cataloging in Publication Data
Brown, Marc Tolon. Pickle things.
SUMMARY: Describes in rhyme the many things a
pickle isn't.
[1. Pickles—Fiction. 2. Stories in rhyme] I. Title.
PZ8.3.B8147Pi   [E]   80–10540
ISBN 0–8193–1027–1   ISBN 0–8193–1028–X lib. bdg.

FOR:
TOLON AND TUCKER
TWO SWEET PICKLES

Pickle things you never see...
Like pickles on a Christmas tree.

A pickle ear,

a pickle nose,

pickle hair,

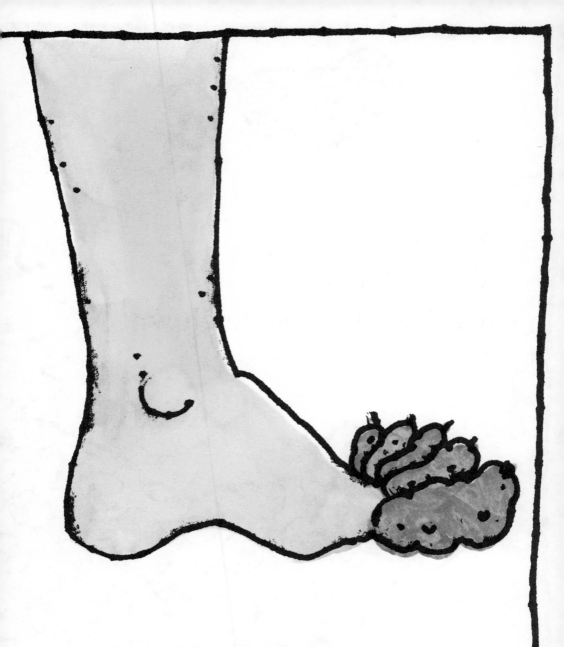

and pickle toes.

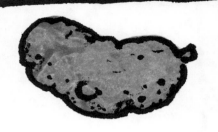

Pickle up,
pickle down,
juggled by a pickle clown.

Pickle in,

pickle out,

pickles from the waterspout.

Pickle
things
you
never
make . . .

Like pickle pie

and pickle cake.

Pickle donuts,

pickle flakes,

pickle candies,

pickle shakes.

Pickle things you never buy...

Like pickle kites
that fly sky high.

A pickle ball,
a pickle bat,

a pickle train,
a pickle hat.

You never hear a pickle talk.

You never see a pickle walk.

You never hear a pickle sing.

Or see a pickle leave a ring.

Can you ride a pickle boat
around a pickle-castle moat?

Or ever steer a pickle bike
down pickle street and pickle pike?

Or ever fly a pickle plane
through pickle snow
and pickle rain?

Or ski a pickle down a slope?

Or
climb
a pickle
with a
rope?

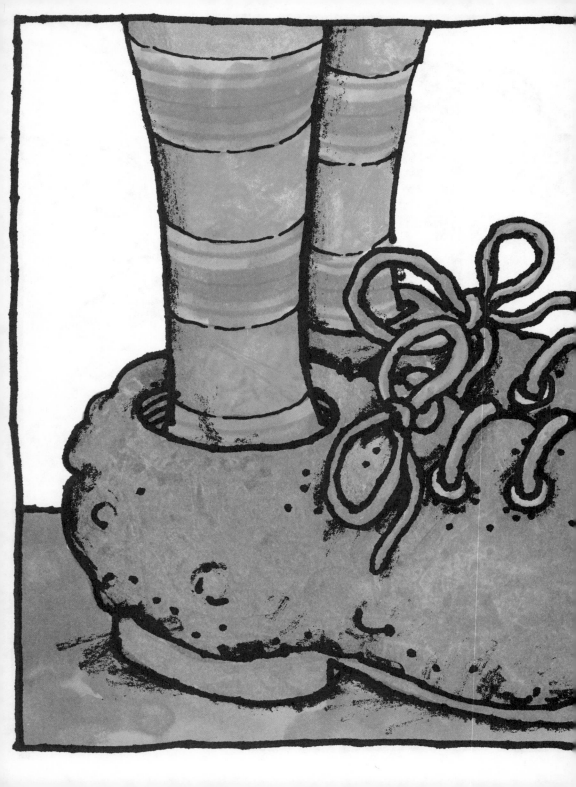

One thing for sure you never do
is wear a pickle for a shoe.
Never pickles on your feet ...

Of course not, silly,
THEY'RE TO EAT!

ABOUT THE AUTHOR/ILLUSTRATOR

MARC BROWN tries out many of his book
ideas on the children he visits in schools
across the country—as well as on
his own two sons. He is always eager
to share their enthusiasm and listen
carefully to their suggestions, which he
feels has helped his growth as a writer
and illustrator.

Mr. Brown first appeared on the Parents
list as illustrator of Judy Delton's
Rabbit's New Rug. He followed that with
Witches Four, his own story, which—
like *Pickle Things*—is in simple,
humorous verse. Marc Brown lives in
Hingham, Massachusetts.